I Love My New Toy!

An **ELEPHANT & PIGGIE** Book

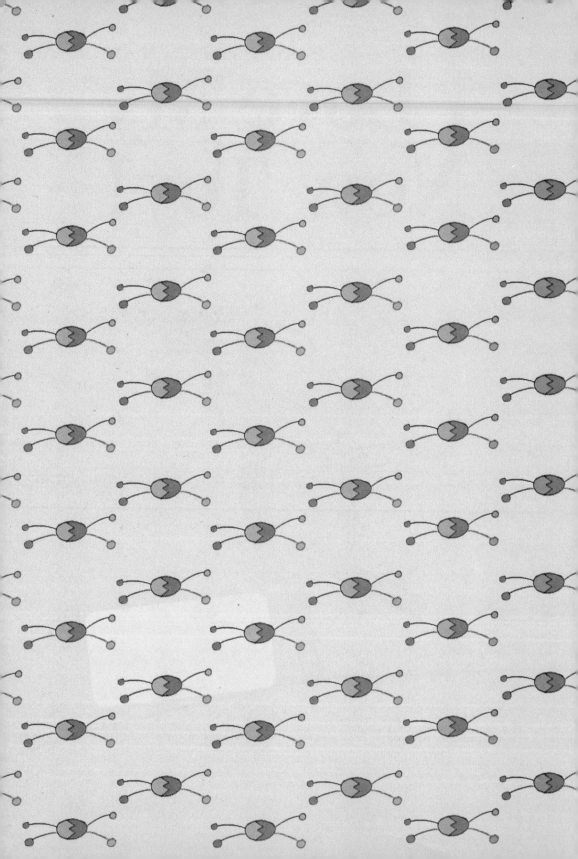

To Lowell, Lee, and Chelsea

ISBN: 978-0-545-23262-3

Text and illustrations copyright © 2008 by Mo Willems. All rights reserved. Published by Scholastic Inc., 557 Broadway, New York, NY 10012, by arrangement with Hyperion Books for Children, an imprint of Disney Book Group, LLC. SCHOLASTIC and associated logos are trademarks and/or registered trademarks of Scholastic Inc.

36 35 34 33 32 31   16 17/0

Printed in the U.S.A.   40

First Scholastic printing, December 2009

I Love My New Toy!

An ELEPHANT & PIGGIE Book

By Mo Willems

SCHOLASTIC INC.
New York Toronto London Auckland Sydney Mexico City New Delhi Hong Kong

Hi, Piggie!
What are you
doing?

2

4

I love my new toy.

What does it do?

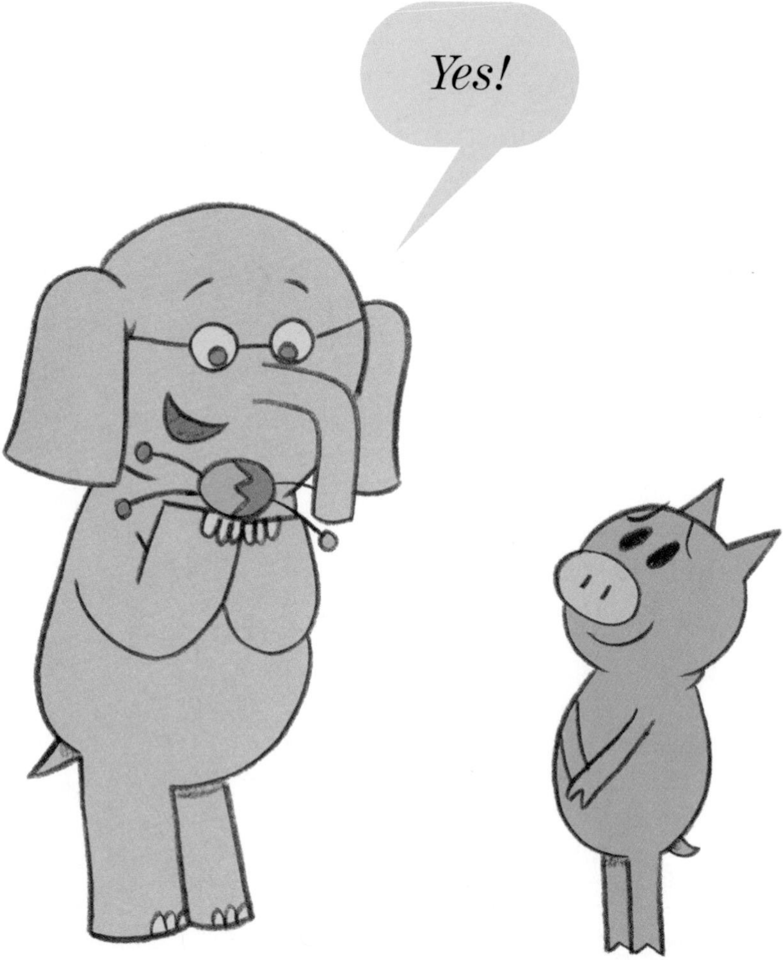
Yes!

Zip!

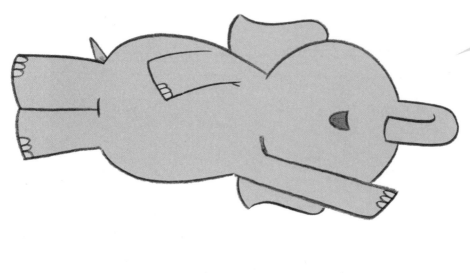

Here it comes!

ZOOM!

Turn

18

21

I broke your toy.

You broke my toy.

31

My new toy
is broken!

AAAAH!

AAAAH!

Cool!

You have a
break-and-snap toy.

SNAP!

Enjoy!

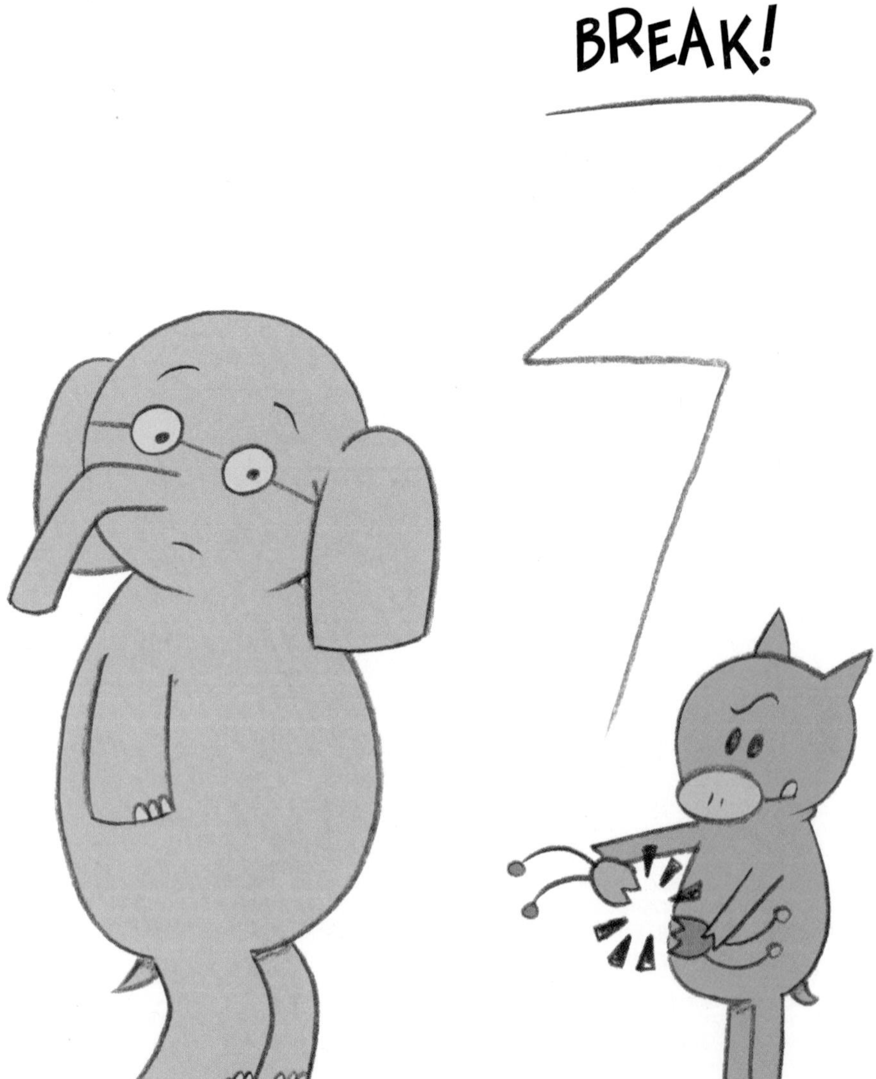
BREAK!

SNAP!

BREAK!

SNAP!

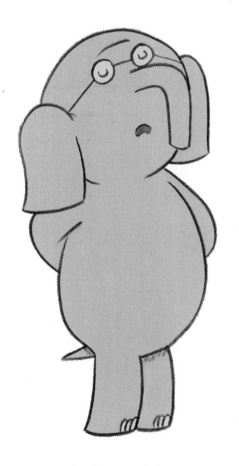

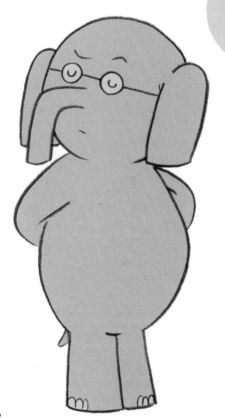

You do not want to play with my new toy?

Friends are more fun
than toys.

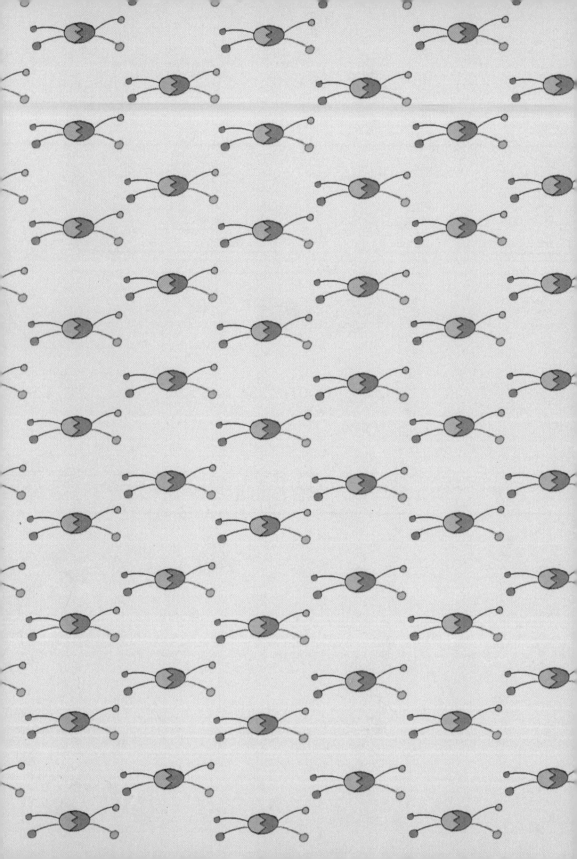